ONE-NIL

ONE

TONY BRADMAN

With illustrations by
Michael Broad

Barrington Stoke

For Oscar – the best footballer I know

First published in 2017 in Great Britain by
Barrington Stoke Ltd
18 Walker Street, Edinburgh, EH3 7LP

www.barringtonstoke.co.uk

This 4u2read edition based on *One-Nil*
(Barrington Stoke, 2008)

Text © 2017 Tony Bradman
Illustrations © 2013 & 2017 Michael Broad

A CIP catalogue record for this book is available
from the British Library upon request

ISBN: 978-1-78112-597-7

Printed in China by Leo

Contents

Chapter 1
Secret Training

"You're kidding," Luke said. "You must be joking!"

"I'm not," said Jamie. "My dad said the full England squad are training at the City ground tomorrow morning."

'Jamie's dad should know,' Luke thought. His job was to look after the pitch at City, the local club. Jamie and Luke were best mates, and they were both in their school's football team. Luke had gone to City with Jamie loads.

1

Jamie could get in any time because his dad worked there.

Luke and Jamie were on their way home from school. When they got to the gates of the park, they stopped. Most afternoons they had a kick-about there. But today they went over to the playground instead.

"My dad says no one's meant to know. It's a big secret," Jamie said.

"They must want to practise some set-piece moves without anyone seeing them," said Luke. "It's the big match next week, isn't it?"

England were due to play France in a World Cup game.

"My dad says I can have the day off to go down and watch them train," Jamie said. "Do you want to come too?"

Luke closed his eyes and dreamed he was standing on the centre spot in a great stadium, waving to the crowd. There was nothing he'd rather do than watch England train – unless it was to pull on a real England shirt, trot out onto the pitch and score a goal. In his mind he saw his hero Steve Browning cross the ball, he heard the crowd roar ...

"I bet your mum won't let you have the day off," Jamie said.

Luke opened his eyes. Jamie was right.

Luke's mum didn't like football. And when it came to time off school, she was very strict. It was no use even asking her.

Luke was really fed up. The England squad were going to be so close. But they might as well be on the moon for all the good it would do him.

But then he had an idea.

"I'll be there, Jamie," he said. "I'm not missing out on this."

There was one thing that might make his mum let him stay away from school. But Luke would need a plan ...

Chapter 2
A Brilliant Plan

Luke's mum was sitting on his bed.

"Are you sure you don't feel well?" she said.

It was the next morning, and Luke hadn't got out of bed. He looked at his mum. He had to make her think that he was ill. Then she'd go off to work and he'd be free to do what he wanted.

"I feel so rough, Mum," he said. That sounded all right – weak, in pain – but not too much.

Mum sat down on the side of the bed and put her hand on his head. Luke could feel the cold metal of her wedding ring on his skin.

"You do feel a bit hot," she said, and she peered into his eyes. "There's a nasty bug going round ..."

"I won't miss much at school," Luke said. "We've got PE and Mr Castle will make us do it outside, even if it rains."

"Right, that settles it," Mum said. "I don't want you outside in the cold and wet. Not in your state. The only trouble is – who's going to look after you? I can't take any time off work, and your sister won't be back from school till this afternoon ..." She thought about it for a minute. "I know, I'll ask Penny – she owes me a favour. I babysat little Tom for her last week."

"That's fine by me, Mum," Luke said. He tried hard not to grin.

"Right, I'll ring her now," Mum said. "You'll be OK on your own for half an hour. It'll take her that long to get here. I'll take you to the doctor's tonight if you're no better."

Luke didn't get out of bed until he heard Mum's car turn the corner and go down the main road. He was grinning now! His plan had worked. All he had to do was phone Mum's friend Penny and stop her coming. And he had a plan for that ...

"Oh, hello, Luke," Penny said when he rang her. "I'm sorry to hear you're not well. I'll be with you as soon as I –"

Luke jumped in before she could go on. "It's OK, you don't have to come now," he said. "Mum forgot – my sister's got study leave today. She just has to pop into school to pick up some books. She'll be back to look after me soon."

"Well, if you're sure," Penny said. "I don't mind."

"We'll be fine, thanks," Luke said. "And I rang Mum on her mobile, so you don't need to tell her, either."

"OK then," Penny said. "Hope you feel better soon ... bye!"

Luke put the phone down and stood there with his eyes closed and his mind full of football scenes. He was scoring goals for England, he was taking a cross from Steve Browning ...

He'd done it. His plan had worked like a dream. He could go and see the England squad train at City.

"Luke – one, Mum – nil!" he said, and went to get ready.

Chapter 3
A Near Thing

Luke took a long time to pick his clothes. He put on his favourite football shirt – the Spurs one with a 10 on the back. He pulled on his football socks, then his jeans. Last of all, he put on his best trainers.

He picked up his football boots too, and went downstairs to the kitchen. Luke hadn't skipped school much before. He was always too worried about what his mum would say if she found out. The house was so still it was almost creepy. Luke could hear the fridge humming and the hall clock ticking, and his own steps seemed extra loud.

Most days the house was full of noise, with Luke's dad shouting for a clean shirt and his mum telling him where the iron was, or his sister with her music on as loud as it would go.

Luke looked at the clock – there would be a bus on the corner in five minutes. He had checked the bus times on his way home last night. He didn't want to miss a second of the England squad's training. He went into the hall, put on his hoodie and stepped outside.

It was raining and Luke had turned to shut the door when he remembered he needed his key. What if he came back and couldn't get in? The thought made him go all hot and sweaty. He nipped back inside, picked up the key and stepped out again.

That had been a near thing! But as Luke shut the door again, he couldn't help laughing to himself. Today was going to be a dream.

Luke was glad of his hood to keep the rain out, but also to make sure none of the neighbours saw him. He ran along the street, sticking close to the hedges and garden walls.

The bus arrived at the corner just as he got there. That was a relief – he wouldn't have to stand around waiting.

Just in case, he'd got his story all ready. If someone stopped him and asked why he wasn't at school he was going to say he was late. And on the way back he'd say he was going home for lunch! Easy!

Luke sat right at the back of the bus, and huddled down. There was no one about and the streets were wet and empty. He saw one old lady and then a mum with a pram, going to the shops.

And then Luke saw a policeman.

He ducked down as fast as he could. Had the policeman seen him?

That was the trouble with skipping school – it was all a bit stressful.

You had to keep away from places where someone from school might spot you, or where someone might know who you were. And if a policeman saw you, he might ask tricky questions.

Luke could feel his heart thumping. He thought his story about being late would fool anyone who stopped him. But how could he be sure?

Luke began to think that skipping school wasn't a very good idea after all. But at least he had somewhere to go – and a chance to see something really exciting.

Luke sat up and peeped out of the window. He couldn't see the policeman any more – but he could see that he was nearly at the City ground. The main stand loomed in front of him.

'Are the England squad inside already?' Luke wondered. He sprang off the bus as soon

as the doors opened. He made for the side gate Jamie had told him to use. Where the players went in ...

"And it's Luke Bennett racing up the wing ..." he said to himself as he ran into the ground. What a day it would be!

Chapter 4
At the Ground

For a terrible moment Luke thought Jamie had been having him on. The ground was empty and still. But as he walked down the touchline he began to hear shouts in the distance. He looked up, into one of the stands across from him, and saw some figures running up and down. A voice floated across the pitch, and an echo went round the ground.

"Put some welly into it, John ... it's no good unless it hurts! Get those knees up, Wayne. Come on, Steve, let's see some effort ..."

They were all there – the full England squad – with the assistant coach, Jimmy Taylor. Luke knew the professionals always started their training with some loosening up and some fitness exercises, perhaps even a run. But this looked like torture. Jimmy Taylor had them all running up the steep rows of seats, up and down and back up again.

Luke walked along the touchline and peered into the stand. It was in shadow, so he couldn't see much. But he could make out some faces he knew even from where he was – faces he'd only ever seen on TV before. And yes, there was Steve Browning ...

"Come on, Steve!" Jimmy Taylor's voice boomed across the ground.

Steve Browning put on a sprint, but then he slowed down.

"Hey, Luke! You made it then!"

Jamie was jogging down the touchline towards him.

"Yeah, I'm ill." Luke grinned. "My mum thinks I'm dying!"

Jamie grinned too. "What will she do if she finds out? Will she give you a really hard time?"

"She's not going to find out, is she?" Luke said. "If she did she'd ban me from football for life."

They started to walk up the touchline. Luke could see a group of men standing near the corner of the pitch up at the other end. He knew who one of them was. Bill Mann – manager of the England team!

Luke had seen Bill Mann on the TV and in the papers, and now here he was, in the flesh, for real. The men around him must be journalists. They were asking questions and every time Bill Mann said anything they wrote it down in their notebooks. A few of them had cameras slung all over them.

Jamie's dad was there too. He saw Luke and Jamie, and called them over. "Luke, Jamie," he said, "meet Bill Mann, manager of the next World Champions."

Bill Mann laughed.

"We'll do our best," he said. He turned to
the two boys and held out his hand. Jamie
shook hands first, and then it was Luke's turn.
The England manager gripped his hand. Luke
couldn't believe all this was really happening!

Chapter 5
A Tough Game

"You a footballer, son?" Bill Mann asked. He'd turned round to have a proper chat with Luke.

"Er ... yes, sir, I mean, I play for the school team, Mr Mann, sir." Luke could feel everyone looking at him, and his cheeks burned red. It was magic – he was talking to the England manager.

"Football's the greatest sport in the world," Mr Mann said. "Do you want to be a professional one day?"

Luke grinned. "Definitely, sir."

"Keep at it, then, son. Keep at it." Mr Mann turned to look as his players made their way onto the pitch. Then he turned back to Luke and smiled again.

"Did school give you the day off to come and watch? Pick up a few ideas for the school team, maybe?"

Luke could feel himself blush even more.

"Er … yes, but, well … not exactly …" He didn't know what to say.

Bill Mann's smile vanished. He started to wag his finger at Luke.

"Tut, tut … you haven't skived off from school, have you?" he said.

"Well …" Luke didn't finish.

"I'll give you a bit of advice, son," Bill Mann said. "Football's a tough game. What happens if you don't make it as a professional? Amateur teams are full of good players who weren't good enough to make it in the League. If you don't make it, you'll need something to fall back on, won't you?"

"Yes, sir, I mean, Mr Mann," Luke stuttered.

"That's right," Mann said. "You'll need some exams. Keep up your school work. It's hard enough getting a job of any sort these days."

Luke blushed from the roots of his hair to the tips of his toes. He didn't know where to look. Everyone seemed to be staring at him – and at Jamie too. But then Bill Mann laughed again.

"Don't take it too hard, son. One day won't make that much of a difference, so long as it is only one day, mind. And so long as you promise me you'll make a special effort at school from now on."

"Oh I will, Mr Mann, I will," Luke promised.

Bill Mann turned to the journalists.

"I used to have the odd day off myself to go and watch Newcastle United train when I was a lad," he said. "My mam nearly killed me when she found out. She still thinks I should have worked harder at school and forgotten about football!"

Everyone else laughed too.

"Well, I'd better make sure the lads are working hard," Bill Mann said. He turned to Luke and Jamie again. "Enjoy your day, boys – and remember what I've said!"

He walked onto the pitch.

And Luke did enjoy his day, every second of it. While the squad was finishing off its fitness training and exercises, he and Jamie had a kick-about at the other end of the pitch. But their eyes kept drifting towards their heroes. At last, Luke and Jamie saw that the squad was going to practise some set-piece moves, and they ran round to watch.

Luke and Jamie stood a few yards to one side of the goal. The England goalie, Peter Sharpe, was already standing on the line.

"Hey up, lads, I wouldn't stand there when Steve Browning takes a shot," he said. "You'd be safer standing in the middle of the goal."

Luke and Jamie laughed. For Luke it was paradise. He was here with his heroes and they were talking and joking with him!

It was great watching the free-kick moves too. They promised Peter Sharpe and the other players that they wouldn't say a word to the French team about England's special plans. Not before the big game. Luke almost felt part of the England squad. He spent most of the morning dreaming about pulling on an England shirt and playing in the World Cup Final.

He could almost feel the ball at his feet, feel the power in his legs as he volleyed the winning goal into the net from 35 yards. He could feel himself punching the sky and turning round for the hugs and shouts of his team mates and the wild cheers of the crowd ...

Chapter 6
Dream Goal

"Hey, you two! Wanna game?"

Luke looked at Jamie, and Jamie looked at Luke. Then they both looked at Steve Browning, who was running towards them from the little group of players in the middle of the pitch. He was grinning.

"Well, do you want a game or not? We're two short for a full side and we need a couple of nifty players."

Luke looked at Jamie again – and Jamie
looked at Luke.

"Yeah!" they both shouted.

And then they were on the pitch, trotting
towards the centre spot, towards Luke's
favourite dream.

"Well, you lot, these two are my secret
weapon," Bill Mann told the players. "They're a

couple of young lads I've been bringing along in secret, and they're going to give you hell. Remember, they're after your places." He winked at Luke and Jamie.

Steve Browning put Luke in midfield, on the right, and Jamie on the left. He laughed and joked with the boys and told them there was no way they'd lose today with Sharpey in goal … And they were kicking off. Luke was playing in a training match with the England squad, and on the same team as his hero, Steve Browning!

It was all like a dream. Everything Luke did went right. He passed well, ran off the ball well, even tackled well, even if he did know none of the squad were trying too hard. There was lots of laughing and joking. Danny Thomson, the Aston Villa midfielder, went flying every time he was on the ball and Luke went near him.

"Ref! That kid's a killer! He's after me all the time!" he moaned.

The ref was Bill Mann, and he was also
playing up front for the other team. He was
panting a bit but he seemed to be having a lot
of fun. And he kept giving Luke advice.

"Easy, take it easy now, son, head up, look
for a spare man now!" he shouted.

When Luke made a good pass, Bill Mann
would run past and tell him he was playing
well. Jamie wasn't having a bad game either.

They were only playing 15 minutes each
way. After they'd changed ends, Luke had the
feeling he always had when he was in a match –
he didn't want it to end. He would have been

happy to play on for days, weeks, months. He dreaded the sound of the final whistle.

Near the end, Luke picked up the ball from Steve Browning just inside the other half. Jamie was to his left, moving towards the area, so he let him have it. Jamie put it straight on to Steve Browning who took it on a speed run to the corner flag – just like in Luke's favourite fantasy!

Luke moved into the area, calling for the ball. Danny Thomson drifted in with him. Steve Browning checked his run near the corner flag, beat his marker, and looked up to see where everyone was.

Luke had his arm up, and he was calling for the ball. He looked at Peter Sharpe on his goal line. Sharpe smiled at him, and then looked out at Steve Browning. Luke saw Browning hit the cross over, and he watched the ball curve over the heads of the defenders. It was coming towards him ...

And then he was running, his eyes still fixed on the ball. Everything seemed to go into slow motion, and there was nothing else in the world but Luke and that ball. He was running faster and faster, he felt both feet leave the ground, he felt where the ball was ... his head connected with it with a THUD! and then he slid over in the mud of the goal mouth and skidded to a stop just near Peter Sharpe.

The world clicked back into being normal again. Luke heard shouts and cheers.

He looked up and the net was still rippling from where the ball had slid down it and into the back of the goal. He'd scored with a beautiful diving header.

He'd scored a goal against the England keeper.

ONE NIL!

Chapter 7
Action Replay

"Great goal, son, great goal!"

Steve Browning helped Luke up off the ground and slapped him so hard on the back that he nearly fell over again.

"You doing anything next Wednesday night? We need a striker," Steve Browning said.

He had his arm round Luke as they walked back to the centre spot. All the other players called out and clapped, and Bill Mann blew

three long, loud blasts on his whistle for the
end of the game.

"Good goal, son," he said to Luke, then he shouted at Peter Sharpe. "And where were you, Sharpey? You should have taken out the cross!"

Luke heard Sharpe's response, but he wasn't really listening. He was stuck in an action replay of his goal. He felt he was walking about two metres above the ground. And he kept on feeling that way until he saw some of the players coming out of their dressing room a bit later to get in their cars and drive off. Bill Mann said he could keep the ball he'd scored with. He had washed and dried it for him so that the squad could sign it. They'd done the same for Jamie with another ball.

One by one the cars started to drive away from the car park, until there was only Bill Mann and a couple of the journalists left.

"Can you sign the ball for me too, Mr Mann?" Luke asked.

"Sure, son." Mr Mann signed in an empty space on the ball. "Now, you remember what I said about your school work. But why don't you come down to one of City's trials in a season or two? They've got a good academy. You could do worse."

And then he got in his car and drove away.

"Hey Jamie, it's been a great day," Luke said.

"Too right," said Jamie. "You've done yourself some favours there, Luke. You'll be playing for England next."

"You weren't too bad yourself," said Luke.

Luke coughed, and coughed again. His throat was a little tickly, and he felt a bit hot and woozy too. But he didn't take much notice. He liked what Jamie had said, but he couldn't tell him about his secret hope – that Bill Mann would remember him.

"Yeah, well, see you," Luke said, and he turned to go home.

Luke sat at the back of the bus home, and looked out at the empty streets. It was just after 1 p.m., and in a few hours the streets would start filling up again with kids coming home from school. They'd had a boring day, the same as any other. But Luke had something to remember.

The only problem was that he couldn't talk about his day to anyone, at least not to his mum or dad. Dad would be over the moon, if he knew. But they'd murder Luke if they found out he'd been skiving off school. He'd have to hide the football he'd got as well, at least until he could think of a good excuse for why he had it. Maybe he'd say Jamie's dad had got it for him. That was it – perfect!

Luke let himself into the still, empty house. He made some toast and had a glass of milk.

His throat felt sore now and he was coughing a lot. He was hotter too, and shivery.

He went upstairs, stuffed his muddy clothes in a bag and shoved them under his bed with the ball. Then he got into bed and fell asleep with a huge smile on his face.

Chapter 8
Big Trouble

Luke didn't remember much more of the afternoon. He didn't remember his sister coming home and peering at him. He didn't remember his mum coming in and putting her hand on his head again, but for a second her ring felt nice and cool on his face. He didn't remember her phoning the doctor, who promised to come in the morning.

When Luke woke the next morning, he felt a little better, but his throat was still sore and it hurt when he coughed. But it didn't seem to matter. He could remember the day before, and the memory of his goal made him smile. He could hear noise from the kitchen, so everyone else was up and about. He knew he wouldn't be able to go to school today. He smiled. It wasn't a skive either, this time.

Just then, his bedroom door opened and his sister poked her head in.

"Who's in big trouble, then?" she said.

"What?" Luke croaked. Too late. His sister had gone. Then the door opened again, and his mum came in, with a newspaper in her hand.

"Well, how's our poor sick boy this morning?" she said.

Luke tried a weak smile. "Er ... I think I feel a bit better," he said.

"I'm glad," Mum said.

She was smiling now, but it wasn't a real smile. It looked nasty. Luke had seen one like it before. His mum smiled like that just before a grade A, number one, total telling-off.

"I thought you might like to read the paper," Mum went on, and she tossed it at him. "Open it, then," she said. "The sports pages."

Luke did as he was told. Then he gulped so hard it hurt his throat. There, in the paper for all to see, was a picture of him standing next to Bill Mann. One of those photographers must have taken it yesterday! There was a headline under the photo, too. "Mann plans for the future." There was also a little story about how 'two schoolboys' had been watching England train at City's ground, and one of them had put a goal past Peter Sharpe in a training match. The journalist had written at the end of the story, "... let's hope Sharpey was only messing about when he got beaten by a kid."

It was a killer. At any other time Luke would have been sky-high with pride. Not only had he played with the England squad and scored a goal – he'd got his picture in the paper! But he was in trouble instead.

Big trouble. He opened his mouth to speak. Mum held up her hand.

"Don't bother," she muttered. "I only hope for your sake that they'll be OK about this at school when they see it – and, trust me, they will see this."

Luke hadn't thought of that. He felt even worse.

"Me and your dad were gobsmacked," Mum went on. "You are never to lie to me like that again. We're the ones who get taken to court if you skive off school, you know. If you ever do it again, I'll ... I'll ..."

Luke's mum sat on the bed and, for a moment, he thought she was going to cry. But she looked up and shook her head – then she smiled.

"You should have heard your dad," she said at last.

"Was he really angry?" Luke said.

"Angry?" his mum said. "He didn't know where to put himself for pride. But he's still going to give you a good telling-off when you're feeling better."

"So you do believe I'm ill today?" Luke said.

His mum looked at him hard.

"I believe you," she said. "Thousands wouldn't."

Luke smiled at her. She stood up and went to the door. She stopped, then turned to look at him once more.

"And your punishment will be ..." she said, "... no pocket money – and no football outside school ... for a month."

"A whole month!" Luke croaked. "But Mum, that's just not fair!"

It was too late. The door shut behind her. Then he heard her laugh, and her last words on the subject floated up the stairs.

"Mum – one, Luke – nil."

If you liked this then you'll love ...

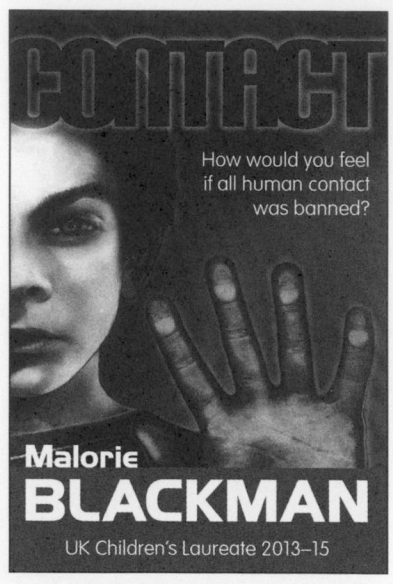

Contact is forbidden

No handshakes. No hugs. Even sport is virtual. But Cal and his mates are tired of playing by the rules ...

A game of two halves ...

Jud's team is 2–0 down in the big
match when their star player is hurt.
Can Jud save the day?

Our books are tested
for children and young people by
children and young people.

Thanks to everyone who consulted on
a manuscript for their time and effort in
helping us to make our books better
for our readers.